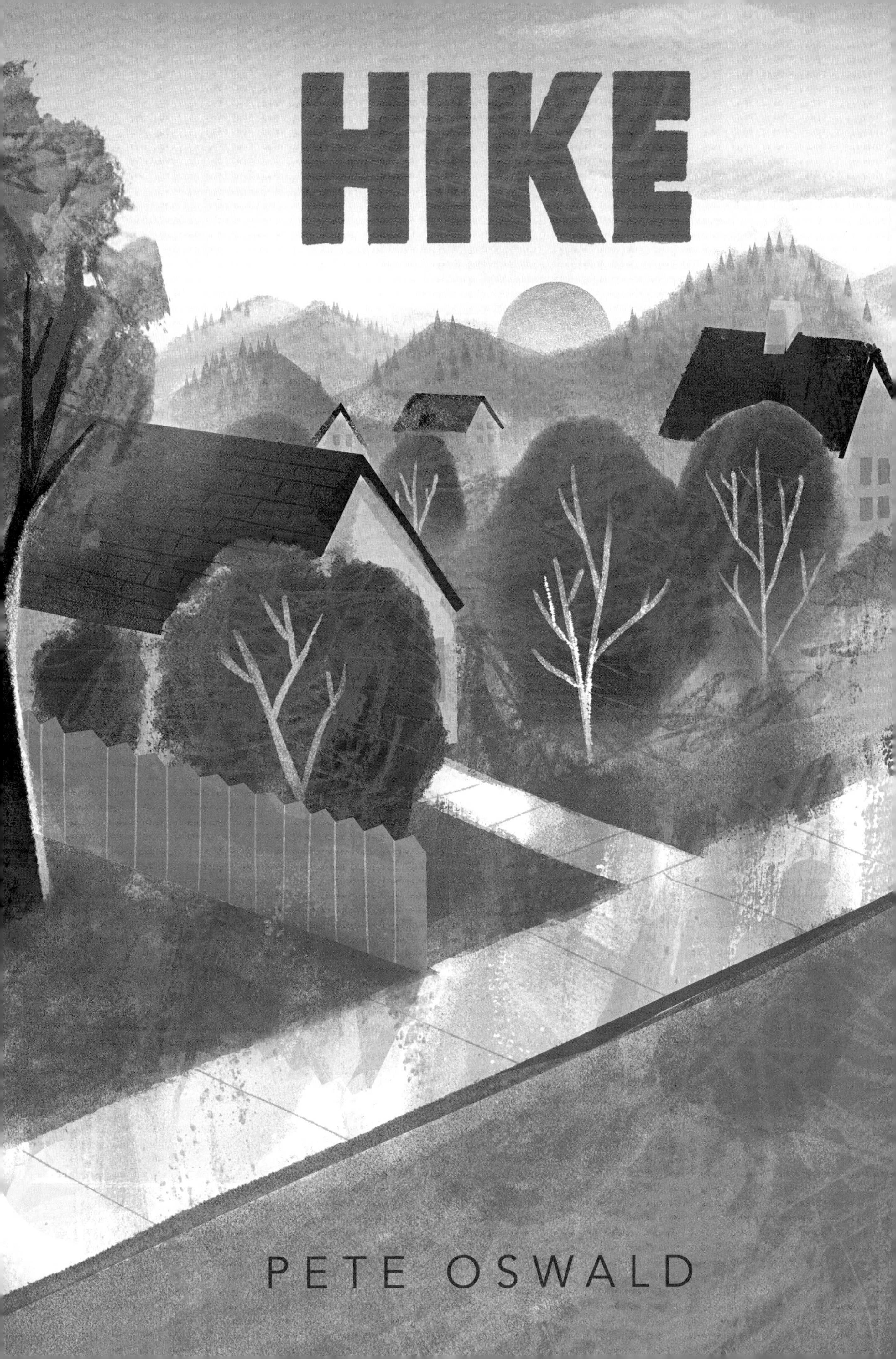
HIKE
PETE OSWALD

MIAOW!

ZIP!

CLICK!

MUNCH!

KNOCK!
KNOCK!
KNOCK!

CLICK!

CHEERS!

PURR

TO DAD AND PAPA

First published 2020 by Walker Books Ltd
87 Vauxhall Walk, London SE11 5HJ

2 4 6 8 10 9 7 5 3 1

© 2020 Pete Oswald

The right of Pete Oswald to be identified as author and illustrator of this work has been asserted
by him in accordance with the Copyright, Designs and Patents Act 1988

This book has been handlettered by Pete Oswald

Printed in China

British Library Cataloguing in Publication Data:
a catalogue record for this book is available from the British Library

ISBN 978-1-4063-9380-4

www.walker.co.uk

WALKER BOOKS
AND SUBSIDIARIES
LONDON • BOSTON • SYDNEY • AUCKLAND